Lift Your Right Arm

Peter Cherches

These five sequences have appeared in whole or in part and in various forms in the the following publications: "Mr. Deadman" in *Fence*, decomP, The Cafe Irreal, and Eclectica; *Bagatelles,* Benzene Editions (1981); "Dirty Windows" in *Between C and D: An Anthology*, Penguin Books (1988); "Trio Bagatelles" in *Conduit*, elimae and MungBeing; and "A Certain Clarence" in *The North American Review.*

ISBN: 978-1-938349-02-7

Library of Congress Control Number: 2012948729

Book and cover design by Mark Givens
Cover drawing from Six Anatomical Tables by Andreas Vesalius.

Printed in the USA

First Pelekinesis Printing 2013

www.pelekinesis.com

Lift Your Right Arm

Peter Cherches

For Nanette Natal, musician and teacher.

Contents

Mr. Deadman

Pushing Up Daisies

You can't keep a dead man down. Six feet under is six feet too many. Dead is fine, dead is dead, but buried is another question, and that question is out of the question, dead or alive, as far as Mr. Deadman is concerned.

So Mr. Deadman plans a getaway, back to the land of the living, and the living dead, if you can tell the difference, that is. Mr. Deadman's been underground way too long.

Now Mr. Deadman figures he'd better get in shape if he wants to bust out. So he starts working out, right there in the coffin. Push-ups and sit-ups. It's pretty cramped in there, and he keeps banging his head on the lid of the coffin, but that doesn't stop him. There's no stopping Mr. Deadman now. He may be dead, but he's not down for the count.

Finally, Mr. Deadman figures he's ready. Good and ready. So he busts through the coffin, into the dirt, the earth, the cold, cold ground. And he pushes his way up, pushes up through dirt, through earth, through ground. And he pushes and pushes, and up he comes, into the air, through the earth, back to earth, down to earth, and what's this he sees? Daisies. Mr. Deadman has literally pushed up the daisies!

Daisies are destiny, Mr. Deadman tells himself. And he begins to pluck the petals. Only this time it isn't "she loves me, she loves me not." This time it's "dead, not dead, dead…"

Variety

Mr. Deadman has experienced a remarkable range of deaths: the quick and relatively painless ones, the long, drawn-out illnesses, the fatal accidents, the brutal murders, and the gentle passing in sleep that most of us yearn for, to name but a few. He considers himself fortunate to have had so many opportunities, so many experiences, to have looked at death from most sides now. Every death is to be treasured in its own way, but the untroubled passing that you and I may wish for doesn't even make Mr. Deadman's top ten.

Death is like a box of chocolates, Mr. Deadman always says. The bittersweet ones are the best.

Another Long Winter

Mr. Deadman can't see his own shadow. In fact, nobody can see Mr. Deadman's shadow. That's because Mr. Deadman casts no shadow.

"Six more weeks of winter," Mr. Deadman pronounces, every Groundhog Day.

The Mirror

Spying Mr. Deadman from afar, in a restaurant or some other public place, you'd be excused if you mistook him for a narcissist. But rest assured, Mr. Deadman is hardly a vain man. If anything, he's the most self-effacing of men. How, then, does one explain the fact that at frequent intervals Mr. Deadman takes a little mirror out of his pocket, seemingly to admire himself?

Easily explained. Mr. Deadman, you see, is not looking at himself in the mirror. It's just that, every now and then, he feels compelled to hold a mirror up to his nose and mouth and then examine it for condensation—because you can never be too sure.

Look-Alikes

In public places, as he attempts to mind his own business, Mr. Deadman is regularly mistaken for someone else. Mr. Deadman has a look-alike, it seems, if not many. "You're his spitting image," strangers tell him, all the time. Or sometimes, "You could be his twin brother," with or without "it's uncanny."

"Of course, he'd be much older," they add, sometimes. "If he were still alive, that is."

The Meaning of Life

Every now and then Mr. Deadman ponders the meaning of life. Sometimes, out of the blue, when he's feeling relatively alive, the fancy just strikes him and he asks himself, "Mr. Deadman, what is the meaning of life?" He racks his brain for an answer, but he never comes up with one. Not that it really bothers him, this lack of an answer, to tell the truth. You live, you die, you live, you die, etcetera, etcetera, ad infinitum, he thinks. In the long run, does it really matter what any of it means?

To ponder the meaning of life, Mr. Deadman realizes, is a luxury reserved for the idle living.

The Mortal Coil

Bitten by the bug of nostalgia, Mr. Deadman goes to his dusty old toy chest and brings out the favorite toy of his youth, and his life, his Slinky. Jiggling the Slinky between the palms of his hands, Mr. Deadman is enveloped by the warm glow of familiarity. The Slinky is the perfect toy, Mr. Deadman thinks, a thing inanimate, yet able to mime so faithfully the force of life. With rapt anticipation, Mr. Deadman goes to the top of the stairs and lets the Slinky loose to do its famous walking down the stairs trick. A child again, Mr. Deadman is transfixed as he watches the Slinky slink its way down the long, long staircase. So transfixed is Mr. Deadman that he suddenly loses his footing and he too begins to descend the staircase. But this is not the graceful walk of a Slinky; this, he knows, is a fatal tumble, pure and simple. Never one to fear death, Mr. Deadman begins to sing:

> To my maker in a coffin
> It's a trip I've taken often
> Here I come sweet soil,
> Off I'm gonna shuffle,
> Shuffle off this mortal coil.

And with those final words, his song now fully sung, at the bottom of the stairs, beside his beloved Slinky, Mr. Deadman expires, returning, once again, to his natural state.

The Revival Theater

Mr. Deadman's favorite films are the old ones, the really old ones, the ones where all the actors are long dead. That's why he goes to the revival theater.

Today, at the revival theater, they're showing a silent film: "Pollyanna." Fabulous, Mr. Deadman thinks. The silent ones are best.

As he watches the film, Mr. Deadman develops a crush on Mary Pickford: young, beautiful, embalmed in celluloid.

Buying the Farm

City living, and city dying, has taken its toll on Mr. Deadman, and now he's ready for the simple life, and an even simpler death. So he buys a farm, a plot of land in the country. He wants to put down roots in the soil.

It's a homecoming of sorts for Mr. Deadman, this return to the soil, though the perspective, this time, from above, is different.

The Personal

Mr. Deadman is feeling lonely, in need of companionship. It's not that he's unused to solitude; he has, after all, experienced the ultimate solitude time and again. Still, everybody needs somebody sometime. For Mr. Deadman, this is the time. He decides to take the bull by the horns and place an ad in the personals.

Mr. Deadman has no idea what to say in the ad. For one thing, what kind of woman is he looking for? He hasn't really given it much thought.

For days, Mr. Deadman obsesses about the ad, composing countless drafts in his head. It is an all-consuming occupation as he racks his brain, trying to figure out just the right language. Finally, he thinks he's come up with something he can live with. He gets a pen and paper and begins to write:

"Wanted: Dead or Alive . . ."

Life

Life, Mr. Deadman says, is a death-defying stunt.

At the Sushi Bar

"Greetings, Deadman-San," the sushi chef says as Mr. Deadman takes a seat at the bar. Mr. Deadman is a regular at this particular establishment. Indeed, all Mr. Deadman has to say is, "The usual," and the chef prepares a combination of his favorite sushi.

Mr. Deadman, a creature of habit, always eats his sushi in the same order. In succession he eats maguro, toro, hamachi, uni, ikura, mirugai, and unagi.

Mr. Deadman has saved the best for last: fugu, poison blowfish. Mr. Deadman appreciates the subtle, delicate flavor, but it is the risk he most enjoys, the culinary flirtation with death. Of course, it is well known that fugu is only served by licensed chefs who are meticulously trained in the art of removing all the poisonous parts from the fish, so in reality the danger is so minuscule as to be illusory.

Mr. Deadman pays the bill and leaves the sushi bar, sated, once again, but unsatisfied, as always, feeling that, however good the food, something was missing.

Tomorrow, Mr. Deadman tells himself, I shall try my luck with mushrooms.

Mr. Deadman Takes a Holiday

Mr. Deadman decides to take a holiday, a holiday from death. Just this once, for a short while at least, Mr. Deadman plans to live life to the fullest. To this end he books a week at a tropical seaside resort.

Mr. Deadman has bought a brand-new wardrobe for this trip, leaving his usual black suit behind. He arrives at the resort clad in a Hawaiian shirt, Bermuda shorts, a Panama hat and sandals. Mr. Deadman has also created a new, temporary identity for himself, beyond the sartorial makeover. He signs the guest register, "Mr. Liveman." For this week "Mr. Deadman" is, for all intents and purposes, dead.

Mr. Liveman is having a ball at the resort. He never imagined life without death could be so much fun. He suns himself on the beach, swims in the ocean, snorkels, gorges himself on the local cuisine and drinks countless Mai Tais, Margaritas, and Piña Coladas.

Then, three days into Mr. Liveman's vacation, disaster strikes. A tsunami hits the coast, killing hundreds, wounding thousands of others, and devastating the resort.

Back home from his truncated vacation, Mr. Deadman reads about the disaster. The newspaper lists the names of the deceased. Among them is a certain Mr. Liveman.

Death on the Installment Plan

Lacking the requisite capital to finance his next death, Mr. Deadman is forced to purchase death on the installment plan. That is, in order to achieve his next full-blown death, Mr. Deadman must first pay for a series of little deaths over time. This will not be so difficult. Mr. Deadman has learned that the French refer to orgasm as *le petit mort*, the little death, so his plan is to buy an orgasm a week for the next year. To this end, Mr. Deadman pays a weekly visit to the bordello of Madame Céline. Each time he chooses a different woman, thinking, variety is the spice of little death, as it is of life. Mr. Deadman never bothers with foreplay. The little death itself is foreplay, he thinks, foreplay to the ultimate death.

Mr. Deadman's weekly visits to the bordello of Madame C are short with but a modicum of sweetness. Mr. Deadman does enjoy the sex, to be sure, but nonetheless, each and every time he returns to life from a little death and considers the rate of interest, he flees Madame Céline's, into the night, convinced he's been taken for a ride.

The Nail Salon

Out for a stroll, one fine day, Mr. Deadman passes a nail salon. A nail salon, Mr. Deadman thinks, just the thing I need! So he enters the salon and says to the receptionist, "I'd like to have my nails done."

"Of course," the receptionist replies. "Just have a seat over there and Julie will take care of you."

Mr. Deadman takes a seat in the manicure chair, his hands in his pockets. "I'd like to have my nails done," he tells Julie.

"Yes, of course, but you'll have to take your hands out of your pockets, sir, so I can see your nails," Julie, the lovely young manicurist, says.

Mr. Deadman removes his hands from his pockets. In each hand is a fistful of rusty iron nails. The nails jangle as Mr. Deadman drops them onto the manicure table.

The lovely young manicurist is taken aback. "What are these?" she asks.

"Doornails," Mr. Deadman replies.

Shuteye

Every life is more exhausting than the last, Mr. Deadman thinks. I could really use a little rest.

Easier said than done. Mr. Deadman has been plagued by insomnia for as long as he can remember, which is longer than you could imagine. For Mr. Deadman it's all or nothing. For Mr. Deadman the big sleep is the only sleep, but right now all he wants is a little shuteye.

The funeral director had assured Mr. Deadman that the coffin was a Perfect Sleeper, but it appears that it's only perfect for the perfect sleep. This time Mr. Deadman just wants to take a nap. Oh, sure he'd like to be dead to the world, but only for an hour or two, this time.

Mr. Deadman slips into his pajamas and hops in his coffin. He tries to make himself comfortable, tries to relax. But thoughts keep racing through his head, thoughts of life and death, and the obligations of both. And then, when he has just about cleared his mind of all cares and woes, the guy in the next coffin over starts snoring, a snore so thunderous it could raise the dead.

Exasperated, Mr. Deadman sits up in his coffin. Eternal rest is such a simple thing, he thinks. But forty winks, forty lousy winks—now that's the killer!

A Stiff

Mr. Deadman does not like being called a stiff. He considers it a slur, a term of disrespect, politically incorrect. Yet the insensitive living don't have the slightest idea how offensive the word "stiff" sounds to the dead. How can they? The dead, after all, are not the type to complain.

Mr. Deadman takes it upon himself set things aright. Any time he hears someone refer to a dead person as a stiff he upbraids them. "You shouldn't use that word," he scolds. "It's a very rude way to refer to the dead." Sometimes he adds, "Dead people have feelings too, you know."

It's no use, unfortunately. These people pay no attention to Mr. Deadman. They look right through him, as if he weren't there.

The Bar

Mr. Deadman's best friend has just died, so they go out to a bar, to celebrate. Neither of them has ever been to this particular bar before. "Welcome to O'Malley's," the bartender says to Mr. Deadman and his friend. "Is this your first time?"

Misunderstanding the question, Mr. Deadman replies, "Yes for him, no for me."

The Dance of Death

Mr. Deadman goes to a dance, a dance of death. All the other dancers are dead too. Mr. Deadman loves going to dances of death. These are my kind of people, Mr. Deadman thinks. I can be myself at a dance of death.

"Shall we dance?" Mr. Deadman asks a woman, a beautiful, well-embalmed woman.

"I'd be delighted," the woman replies, and they dance a minuet.

"This is so much fun," the woman tells Mr. Deadman. "I haven't danced a minuet in ages."

"Nor I," Mr. Deadman replies, "but when you've been dead long enough everything comes back eventually."

Keeping Up With the Joneses

Mr. Deadman is an avid reader of the obituaries, and of late he has noticed an inordinate number of Joneses cropping up. The death notices are chock full of Joneses, positively bursting at the seams with them. What gives? Jones, to be sure, is a common name, yet for some reason the numbers of dead Smiths and Johnsons, equally common surnames, pale by comparison with the Joneses. And what about the Deadmans? Why, if it weren't for Mr. Deadman himself you'd never see that name in the obits at all. Mr. Deadman is enraged. No matter how many times he dies, he just can't keep up with the Joneses.

In an effort to correct the imbalance, Mr. Deadman devotes his life to saving the lives of others—as long as their name is Jones, that is.

Habeas Corpus

Mr. Deadman serves a funeral parlor with a writ of habeas corpus. "A writ of habeas corpus," says the funeral director, examining the document, "I've never heard of such a thing in all my years in this business. What's this all about?"

"A terrible injustice has been done," says Mr. Deadman. "The man you're about to bury hasn't been given a proper trial."

"Trial?" says the funeral director. "What are you talking about? This man died peacefully in his sleep."

"How can you be certain?" asks Mr. Deadman.

"That's how the man's family put it," the funeral director replies. "He died peacefully in his sleep. Those were the exact words."

"Well, I demand a proper trial. If he died peacefully in his sleep it will come out at the trial."

Exasperated, the funeral director asks Mr. Deadman, "And just what is your relationship to the deceased?"

"Self," Mr. Deadman replies.

A Dead Ringer

"Ralph!" a man on the street calls to Mr. Deadman. Mr. Deadman does not respond. "Ralph, don't you remember me?" the man asks.

"You've made a mistake," Mr. Deadman replies. "My name is not Ralph."

"Wow, I'm sorry. You really do look like Ralph," the man says. "It's uncanny how much you look like him. I apologize if I've bothered you, but you're a dead ringer."

"No need to apologize," Mr. Deadman replies. "To be called a dead ringer is an honor indeed."

The man on the street is perplexed but relieved that the stranger has not taken offense.

A Kiss Before Dying

Certain, once again, that his time is up, Mr. Deadman would like a kiss before dying, one last kiss, one more time. So he goes to the carnival, to the kissing booths. Mr. Deadman has been here before. In fact, he's a regular.

There are quite a number of kissing booths at the carnival, staffed by all manner of women, a woman for every taste. All the women recognize Mr. Deadman, and they greet him as he strolls by their booths, hoping for a little business. But, just like every other time, Mr. Deadman passes most of them by. He passes the cute girls-next-door, a dime a dozen at kissing booths. He passes the sexy vixens and the various and sundry other hot numbers. He passes the stunning and elegant fashion-model types. They all have their allure, Mr. Deadman acknowledges, but none of them have the power. So Mr. Deadman heads straight for the kissing booth of Big Bertha, a gargantuan woman who doubles as the carnival's fat lady, the only kisser at the carnival, he knows, who has the power to take away the breath of life, to bestow the kiss of death.

He ponies up his cash, many times the other women's prevailing rate, and Bertha stuffs the wad of bills in her massive cleavage. Then she leans forward, puts her lips to Mr. Deadman's, and lets loose with the mother of all kisses. Mr. Deadman crumbles to the ground. The medics are called, but it's too late. Mr. Deadman is D.O.A.

As the medics load Mr. Deadman onto the stretcher, Bertha winks at the corpse and calls out, "Come back and see me some time, honey," certain, once again, that he will.

A One-Day Sale

Mr. Deadman learns that his favorite coffin showroom is having a one-day sale. Perfect, Mr. Deadman thinks. This couldn't have come at a better time. I've been running low.

At the coffin showroom, the salesman recognizes Mr. Deadman. "Back again so soon?" the salesman asks.

"Well, you know how one runs through these things," Mr. Deadman replies.

"Indeed," the salesman replies, perhaps humoring him. "So what can I show you today? Something in mahogany? Oak? I have some beautiful numbers with gold handles."

"No, no, nothing like that for me," Mr. Deadman says. "Much too fancy. A plain pine box is more my style."

"Indeed," the salesman says, thinking "cheapskate." He gets a pine box from the storeroom and begins to package it for transport.

"Don't bother," Mr. Deadman says. "I'll wear it home."

Bird Lives!

Mr. Deadman notices some faded graffiti on the side of a building in his neighborhood, scrawled in large red capital letters, but barely visible, as time and the elements have taken their toll: BIRD LIVES! This message dates back to the 1950s, after the death of Charlie Parker, the great jazz saxophonist whose nickname was Bird. BIRD LIVES! was ubiquitous for a time, started by a fan and picked up by others until the slogan appeared on walls all over New York and other cities. BIRD LIVES! reminds Mr. Deadman of that other famous graffiti of days gone by, Kilroy Was Here, and its funny little drawing. Mr. Deadman served in WWII with Kilroy and he saw Bird perform at the Onyx Club on 52nd Street a few years later. But graffiti notwithstanding, Bird is dead and Kilroy is no longer here.

Mr. Deadman crosses out Bird's name and replaces it with his own.

Mrs. Deadman

There was a Mrs. Deadman, once, many years ago. Mr. Deadman was utterly devoted to her. She was his everything—his life and his death. They were so in love that they removed the words "till death do us part" from their wedding vows. Death, they knew, could never part them. Their two hearts beat as one. When they beat, that is.

Whether they were together or apart, she was always in Mr. Deadman's thoughts. Sometimes, late at night, when he couldn't die, he'd just watch Mrs. Deadman lying immobile, rigor mortis beginning to set in, and think, I don't know what I'd do without her.

This idyllic marriage lasted many years. Then, one day, Mr. Deadman received a crushing blow that put an end to the spell she had cast over him, and to their marriage. He discovered that Mrs. Deadman was cheating on him. This was not hearsay or rumor. No, it was far worse—he saw it with his very own eyes. And he wished, at that moment, that he were blind. One gray, cloudy day, while strolling through the cemetery, Mr. Deadman caught her in the act. Mrs. Deadman was leaving flowers on another man's grave.

The Museum of Death

A new museum has recently opened in Mr. Deadman's town, The Museum of Death. Mr. Deadman is beside himself with joy to learn of the museum's existence. A museum of death, he thinks, what fun! Mr. Deadman plans a visit, anticipating all the marvels he expects to see: exhibits on funerary rituals throughout history, embalming demonstrations, mummies, extravagant and lavish coffins, death masks of the powerful and famous, and surely some paintings by Goya, Bosch and Ensor—he can only imagine the wonders to be found in The Museum of Death.

But when Mr. Deadman goes to the museum he encounters something completely different. There is nothing at all of what he had expected. Instead, the entire museum is a hall of mirrors, reflecting Mr. Deadman back at himself as he gazes upon the walls. Is Mr. Deadman upset, disappointed? Hardly. In fact, he spends hours in the museum, going from room to room, looking at the mirrors, looking at himself, looking at death. After some time, Mr. Deadman realizes he's the only visitor in the museum.

Mr. Deadman goes up to a guard and says, "This is a fabulous museum. How come there aren't any other visitors?"

"Well, people did come at first, a fair number, actually, but mostly they'd take a quick look around, become confused, or angry, or both, and then they'd demand their money back."

Philistines, Mr. Deadman thinks.

All Roads Lead to Rome

Mr. Deadman stops dead in his tracks and wonders whether he has chosen the wrong direction in life. He considers this dilemma only briefly, however, quickly deciding it's a non-issue. In matters of life and death, Mr. Deadman realizes, all roads lead to Rome, as the saying goes, so he picks up where he left off, continuing in the direction of death, the Rome toward which we're all headed, taking in whatever roadside attractions he happens upon along the way.

Looking Over the Precipice

Mr. Deadman pays a visit to his favorite scenic spot, a steep, perilous cliff. Mr. Deadman loves to walk up to the edge and peer over. Every time he sees something different.

A Barbecue Death

In his latest death, Mr. Deadman dies by barbecue. This is a death that Mr. Deadman has been looking forward to for a long, long time. He started seasoning himself for this death quite a while ago.

When the time finally comes, however, Mr. Deadman realizes that he has neglected one very important detail concerning the manner of his death: smoked or not smoked, and if smoked, hickory or mesquite? It may be many, many deaths before the barbecue opportunity knocks again, so Mr. Deadman wants this one to be just right. But what is right, after all? It's all just a matter of taste, and a tasteful death is the best death of all.

Well, I do think barbecue is best when smoked, Mr. Deadman thinks, and I've always preferred hickory to mesquite, so there you have it, I've made my choice: on chips of hickory I shall go. And with that final detail settled, Mr. Deadman hurls himself onto the grill.

A barbecue death may be the greatest death of them all. To be the chef, the diner and the dinner: this is the oneness of which Mr. Deadman has always dreamed.

Bagatelles

Lift your right arm, she said.

I lifted my right arm.

Lift your left arm, she said.

I lifted my left arm. Both of my arms were up.

Put down your right arm, she said.

I put it down.

Put down your left arm, she said.

I did.

Lift your right arm, she said.

I obeyed.

Put down your right arm.

I did.

Lift your left arm.

I lifted it.

Put down your left arm.

I did.

Silence. I stood there, both arms down, waiting for her next command. After a while I got impatient and said, what next.

Now it's your turn to give the orders, she said.

All right, I said. Tell me to lift my right arm.

Her voice. It ruled me. Not she, not by any measure. But her voice, when it chose to speak to me.

She was a constant. I used her to gauge reality. The world existed for me in relation to her. For instance, I used her as a standard for temperature. For the sake of convenience, I called her body temperature zero. For us to be comfortable, room temperature had to be considerably below zero. And when she had a fever it had to be even colder.

I often told myself, were it not for her I would be alone. I often told myself, were it not for me she would be alone. I often told myself, one should not be alone. I often told her, one should not be alone. I often asked myself, could I live without her. I often asked her, could you live without me. She often said yes, she often said no.

Yes, I told her, yes, if that's what you'd like. Yes, she said, I would like it, I would like it very much. Very well then, I said, if that's what you'd like, if that's what you'd like then most certainly. Most certainly that's what I'd like, she said, most certainly I'd like that very much. Very well, I said, most certainly, yes. Oh thank you, she said, thank you very much.

Sniffing each other was our favorite pastime. We would produce various and sundry odors for each other's benefit. Some of our odors were mutual, but certainly not all. She produced many odors that I could not duplicate, and vice-versa. We spent many pleasant hours producing odors for each other. When we became familiar with each other's repertoire of odors, we began to make requests. It was pure ecstasy. When we were sniffing each other nothing else mattered. We had each other, and as far as we were concerned, who cared how the world smelled.

You take a lot out of me, she said to me.

I know, I told her in her own voice.

I hear a noise, she said. I don't, I said. I definitely hear a noise, she said. I don't, I said. You must be deaf, she said. Describe the noise, I said. I can't, she said. What does it sound like, I said. I understood you the first time, she said. And, I said. And I can't describe what it sounds like, she said. Show me then, I said. She did. I don't hear a thing, I said. You must be deaf, she said. Try again, I said. She did. Well, she said. I still don't hear a thing, I said. You only hear what you want to hear, she said.

Where is she, I wondered, when she wasn't there. If she's not here she could be anywhere. She could be anywhere and not alone.

I began to imagine the worst. At every imagining I thought I had imagined the worst, then I imagined something even worse. It got to the point where my imaginings no longer included her. I realized that the worst did not encompass her. As my imaginings continued, as worst superseded worst, making the preceding worst only worse, I began to forget her. As worst got worse, I forgot her more. Things were getting pretty bad, and I had almost forgotten her completely, when she reappeared.

Our life together has its limits, I said.

What exactly do you mean, she said.

Our life together is limited in time and space, I said.

Oh, she said.

I said something that she obviously misinterpreted, because she reacted angrily. She was screaming, in a frenzy. I couldn't get a word in edgewise. I let her go on until she ran out of steam. When I was sure she was through, I repeated my original statement. She must have understood this time because she said, oh yes, now I understand.

I had a dream. About her. I dreamed that she wasn't there. Only I was there. I was there, knowing that she wasn't there. I was dreaming knowing that she wasn't there. She wasn't there and I knew it. I dreamed knowing it. I woke up thinking it. But she was there. I saw that she was there. We were both there. I was there, awake, knowing that she was there. And she was there, asleep, dreaming.

Once, while I was licking her, she disappeared. I knew she had disappeared because my tongue was lapping at the air. I was distressed, but I kept on licking. I licked for some time, until I felt her body once again on my tongue.

Let me do your portrait, I said. All right, she said.

She sat for me.

I didn't have a pen. All I had was a blank sheet of paper.

I looked at her, and then at the paper. I looked at the paper for a while, then back at her. Then back at the paper. Back at her. At the paper. Her. The paper. I looked at the paper for some time, then I showed it to her.

It doesn't look anything like me, she said.

It's an idealization, I said.

You're ugly, I told her. Yesterday you said I was beautiful, she said. Yesterday you were beautiful, I said. And today, she said. Today you're ugly, I said.

The next day I told her she was beautiful. Yesterday you said I was ugly, she said. Yesterday you were ugly, I said. And today, she said. Today you're beautiful, I said.

The day after that I told her she was ugly. Yesterday you said I was beautiful, and the day before you said I was ugly, and the day before that you said I was beautiful, she said. Yesterday you were beautiful, two days ago you were ugly, and three days ago you were beautiful, I said. And today, she said. Today you're ugly, I said.

The following day I told her she was ugly. You told me I was ugly yesterday too, she said. Pardon me, I said, I forgot what day it was.

There's something missing from our relationship, she said.

Do you know what it is, I said.

It could be anything, she said.

We had been together for some time by this time. Many years. We had stopped counting. We celebrated anniversaries, but as far as we were concerned each anniversary meant just another year. We kept records, of course, and had we wanted to know we could certainly have looked it up, but neither of us ever did. Sometimes, however, the subject did come up. This was inevitable. For instance, we'd have a fight and she would say, it's been many years, hasn't it. And I, still in the spirit of combat, would say, yes, many, indeed. Or, feeling a bit nostalgic she would say, it's been many years, hasn't it. And I, caught up in the spirit of nostalgia, would say, yes, many, indeed. And, occasionally, simply musing about time and the two of us, she would say, it's been many years, hasn't it. And I, similarly musing about the two of us and time, would say, yes, many, indeed. It's been many years.

You're a prick, she said. You're a cunt, I said. You're a prick, she said. You're a cunt, I said. You're a prick, she said. You're a cunt, I said. I forgot what we're arguing about, she said. Pricks and cunts, I said.

We decided to try something new.

Afterwards, I asked her what she thought.

It seemed familiar, she said. Are you sure we've never done that before.

Positive.

It seemed so familiar. I think we did something like it a long time ago.

I know what you're thinking of, I said. But it wasn't exactly the same thing.

I had nothing to be afraid of. There was only one of her, but there were two of us.

We were going over snapshots, having decided to look back at the past. As we never had a camera, we only had the snapshots of memory. We passed them between us.

Remember this one, she would say, and tell me what she was thinking of. Ah, yes, I would reply with a smile. How about this one, I would say, and tell her mine. Do I ever, she would say, and laugh. We went over hundreds of these pictures, and what memories they brought back. At one point, though, she brought up one that I couldn't seem to place. I don't remember that one, I told her. She thought about it for a few moments and then said, no, come to think of it, neither do I.

She was lying motionless. I went over and kicked her, not too hard, just hard enough to see if she was still alive. She was, because she moved in a certain way. That's good, I thought, because if she's still alive it means that we can resume.

I sat for a while and she walked. Then she got tired and sat, so I walked. I walked for a while, then I told her I wanted to sit, so she got up and walked again. I sat there, watching her walk, remembering how we used to walk together.

We tried to put each other into words. But words weren't enough. So we put each other into sentences. No good. Paragraphs. Unsatisfactory. Chapters. Not quite right. A book. Books. Volume upon volume upon volume. It just wouldn't work. Nothing was enough, everything was too much.

I created you out of nothingness and I can annihilate you any time I feel like it, I told her.

I'd like to see you try, she said.

Dirty Windows

They met at a bookstore. She was thumbing through *Finnegans Wake* when he came by and said, "Nice weather." She liked that, so when he asked her to join him for a cup of coffee she agreed. They started talking and he learned that she was a meteorologist.

Early on in their relationship they agreed to proceed cautiously, so they hired extras to do the stunts.

They went to a motel for couples only. The sign in front promised erotic videos in each and every room, but when they tried the TV all they were able to get was a medical documentary titled "Strep Throat."

"I didn't come here for culture," he said, annoyed.

"What do you think we should do?" she asked.

"Well, we already paid our money," he said, "so let's go to sleep."

He went to take a look out the window. "Boy, your windows are dirty," he told her.

"My windows are clean," she said defensively. "It's your mind that's dirty."

He was watching her sing "The Star-Spangled Banner," one of the later stanzas, the one that begins, "Oh thus be it ever." She was having trouble with the high notes. Then the doorbell rang. He ran to answer it, forgetting to put his pants on. It was a couple of Jehovah's Witnesses, a man and a woman.

"Armageddon will be a happy time," the woman said, ignoring his erection.

"I called you," she said, "but I got a message. It was in your voice and it said, 'You have reached a nonworking number.' I didn't know what to do, so I hung up."

"Was there a beep?" he asked.

"A beep?"

"Yes, a beep. After the message."

"I think so."

"You should have left a message," he said.

He was dreaming that she was telling him that if he didn't stop dreaming about her she would wake him up when he woke her up.

They were singing "One Hundred Bottles of Beer on the Wall" when halfway through they forgot the lyrics.

She was giving him a haircut when he started whistling. It was a strange tune, unlike anything she had ever heard before. She asked him about it and he explained that he used to be an anthropologist, and that he had spent many years in a far-off land studying a most remarkable people who whistled these strange and beautiful songs while they made love. She was so engrossed in his story that she cut off all his hair.

He was imagining he was making love to another woman when he opened his eyes only to discover that she was another woman imagining she was making love to him.

"Your windows are dirty," she said to him.

"It's not my windows," he replied. "It's the world outside."

"Why are you doing this to me?" he asked her.

"Because I want to hurt you," she said.

"There are better ways to hurt me," he told her, and he showed her what they were.

They went to a Halloween party as each other. The costumes were so good that nobody knew who they were.

It was a very large room and they had trouble hearing each other. So when he said, "I have a few things to do. I'll be going out for a while. I should be back in about an hour," she thought he said, "I lost my job and I owe everything we've got to a very big man. I've met another woman and I'm leaving you. Don't try to stop me."

They each placed an ad in the personals for a third party to join them. They were disappointed when they showed up to answer each other's ad.

She was taking a correspondence course in microsurgery. For assignment number three she had to cut him up into little pieces and put him back together. When she told him, he said, "Forget it."

"I realize you're still upset about assignment two," she said, "but I assure you I'll do better this time."

He didn't say a thing. He just put his feet in his pockets and shook his head.

They had made a self-immolation pact, but he got cold feet and chickened out.

He couldn't get used to the new color she had painted the walls. It was a different kind of off-white, similar to the previous shade, but somehow disconcertingly different. He couldn't explain what it was that bothered him, but it bothered him. In fact, it made his skin crawl.

"Why couldn't you use the same color?" he asked her.

"They didn't have any more," she said.

"You should have gone to another store."

"It wouldn't have done any good," she said. "The man told me that the color was discontinued. That this one was the closest thing."

After a moment of silence he said, "The closest thing—that's it!"

She read in a newspaper that he had been taken hostage in the Middle East. She was very angry, so she confronted him. "You don't tell me anything," she said, shoving the paper in his face. "I have to read it in the news."

"What's this?" he asked her, showing her the letter he had discovered.

"It's a love letter from another man," she told him.

"Then why is it in my handwriting?" he asked angrily.

"We did that to trick you," she told the other man.

They always used to take showers together until one day, when they couldn't agree on the temperature.

He couldn't find the thing he was looking for. He looked everywhere. He was getting frustrated. Where was she? She'd know. He kept looking. He went through all the drawers. He even tried using a magnifying glass. No luck. Where the hell was she? He sat in the armchair and waited. When she returned several years later he said, "Where the hell were you?" She didn't say a word. She handed him a small package. It was gift-wrapped. He opened it. Inside the box was a new one, even nicer than the one he had lost.

She had changed. She looked different to him. Odd, but she looked like him. It finally dawned on him what had happened—she had replaced herself with a mirror. So he did the same thing. Replaced himself with a mirror. Then he stood back and watched.

"The human mind is like an attic," he told her.

"Yes, I know," she replied. "And I wish you'd get your junk out of mine."

"How is it outside?" she asked.

"I don't know," he said. "Let me look." He went to the window. "It's sunny," he said and walked away.

She went to look for herself. "It's not sunny," she said. "It's cloudy."

After she had walked away from the window he went back to take another look. "You're crazy," he said. "It's sunny." And he walked away.

She went back to the window. It was cloudy.

This went on for some time. They took turns looking out the window. Every time he looked it was sunny, every time she looked it was cloudy. They finally decided that the only way to settle the matter once and for all was for both of them to look out the window at the same time. So they did. It was night.

They had a famous painter do a double portrait. When he had finished, the painter asked, "Well, how do you like it?"

"It's a good likeness of him," she said, "but it doesn't look anything like me."

"And how do you feel about it?" the painter asked him.

"Well," he replied, "I think it's an excellent likeness of her, but I must say it doesn't look a bit like me."

The painter smiled and said, "I painted you as you see each other."

Trio Bagatelles

One: It's a beautiful day.

Two: You call this a beautiful day?

One: Yes, you don't think it's a beautiful day?

Two: Hardly.

Three: Well, it is a sunny day, I'll grant you. And it's 72 degrees, and the humidity is very low.

One: I'd certainly call that a beautiful day.

Three: I'm not sure beautiful is the right word. Lovely, maybe.

Two: Lovely I could live with.

One: Lovely you could live with, but not beautiful? Is there such a difference?

Two: Enough.

One: You know, you're really a pain in the ass. Both of you.

Two: Pain in the ass! Look who's talking! Beautiful day!

One: I don't care what you say, it's a beautiful day, and I'm going to tell everyone.

Two & Three: Go ahead, tell them.

One: All right, I will. It's...It's...It's a lovely day!

One: Quick! Somebody call the police!

Two: What's happening?

Three: Are you in danger?

One: A crime is being committed!

Two: Yes, but what's the nature of the crime?

One: The nature of the crime?

Three: Yes, what's the offense?

One: Offense?

Two: I don't see any crime being committed.

Two & Three: What do you know that we don't know?

One: This city is overrun with crime. Any time of day a crime is being committed. Call the police!

Two: I think the police are aware of the crime problem.

Three: Without a specific crime to respond to, and a specific location, there's not much the police can do.

One: You're probably right. But one can never be too vigilant. Quick! Call an ambulance!

One: I've decided to go back to school.

Two: How come?

One: I'm sick of my job. I need a career change.

Three: So what are you going to study?

One: I haven't decided yet, but I've narrowed it down to court stenography, podiatry and phrenology.

Two & Three: Phrenology!

Two: Do they still teach that?

One: There's a correspondence course.

Three: That sounds a little risky. Anyway, I'd stay away from phrenology and podiatry if I were you. With phrenology you have to touch heads and with podiatry you have to touch feet.

Two: Yes, and you hate to touch people.

One: You're right. I hadn't thought of that.

Three: So you might as well go ahead and study court stenography.

One: I guess so, but there is that little matter of the law.

Two & Three: Ah, the law!

One: Did you hear the news?

Two & Three: What news?

One: The world is coming to an end.

Two: Where did you hear that?

One: A man and a woman. They came to my door and told me. I think they were selling magazine subscriptions. I don't know why I should subscribe to any magazines if the world is coming to an end. Who knows how many issues I'd actually get.

Three: Those were Jehovah's Witnesses.

One: So? What do I care if they're Jehovah's Witnesses?

Three: That's why they came to your door.

One: Because they're Jehovah's Witnesses?

Three: Yes, that's what Jehovah's Witnesses do. They come to doors.

Two: That's the truth.

One: All right, so Jehovah's Witnesses come to doors. Anyway, one of them told me the world is coming to an end.

Three: Which one told you that?

One: The woman. Why?

Three: I knew it! It's almost always the woman who tells you the world's going to end.

Two: They do that to soften the blow. They think it won't be so scary if a woman says it.

One: Come to think of it, she said it in a soothing, maternal voice.

Three: Yup, that's the Jehovah's Witness M.O, all right. Tell you the world's going to end in a soothing, maternal voice.

One: So is it?

Three: So is what?

One: Is the world going to end?

Two & Three: Who the hell knows!

Three: What did you say?

One: Me? I didn't realize I could be heard.

Three: I could hear that you were saying something, but I couldn't hear what it was.

One: Better that way.

Two: Well, you're certainly being secretive.

One: I said it under my breath. It was something I was thinking. I really shouldn't have spoken at all. It was just a thought. It just slipped out. It wasn't meant to be heard. I was thinking out loud.

Three: Come on, tell. I'm curious.

One: And you? Are you curious too?

Two: I confess. I'm curious. So tell us.

One: All right, if you insist. I said, "So that's where I left it!"

Three: Left what?

One: I didn't say.

Three: Yes, but what was it?

Two: Yes, come on, tell us. What was it?

One: You asked what I said. I told you. But my thoughts? My unspoken thoughts? No. Sorry. That's where I draw the line.

∞

One: I'm sorry.

Two: What are you sorry for?

One: I'm apologizing in advance.

Three: What for?

One: For whatever. For whatever I may do or say that I'll need to apologize for.

Two & Three: You can't do that!

One: Why not? I know I'm going to do something I'll need to apologize for sooner or later, so why not get the apology out of the way?

Three: You just can't do that. It's like giving yourself diplomatic immunity.

Two: Or blanket amnesty.

One: What immunity? What amnesty? I'm apologizing, aren't I? And in any case, I'd certainly apologize after the fact for whatever I did that required an apology, so why can't I just apologize in advance? Either way I'm apologizing.

Two: Yes, but do you mean it?

Three: Yes, is it a heartfelt apology?

One: Yes, it is. It's a heartfelt apology.

Two & Three: How do we know?

One: Take my word.

Two: That's not good enough.

Three: No, you'll have to do better.

One: All right. I'm so sorry. I'm a really thoughtless person. I'm not worthy of your friendship. I'll totally understand if you never want to see me again. All I can say is

---

I'm suffering horribly, and I hope you can see it in your hearts to forgive me.

Two: That's better.

Three: Yes, much better.

Two & Three: We accept your apology.

One: I'm starving.

Two: Literally starving?

Three: Wasting away to nothingness?

Two: On death's doorstep?

One: No, just very hungry. I haven't eaten a thing since this morning. And all I had then was a single Weetabix.

Two: You shouldn't say, "starving," then. It minimizes the true suffering of the millions of people around the world who really are starving.

One: Oh, give me a break! It's a figure of speech. Everybody uses it.

Three: Well, maybe it's time to change that.

Two: Yeah, can't you just say, "I'm hungry"?

One: "Hungry" doesn't really convey the intensity. "Hungry" is subject to interpretation. Just how hungry? "Starving" forcefully and colorfully communicates the message that I'm really dying to eat, and pronto.

Three: You're not really "dying" to eat, you know. If you were literally dying to eat you'd be literally starving. Anyway, "starving" is subject to interpretation just as much as "hungry," don't you think?

Two: When you say, "I'm starving," you scare us. How do we know your life isn't in imminent danger?

One: Tone of voice. Facial expression. There are all sorts of clues. Why are you giving me such a hard time? I just want something to eat. Can I please get out of here?

Three: All right, but just one more thing.

One: What's that?

Three: Did you say you ate a Weetabix this morning?
One: Yes.
Two: With milk?
One: Yes.
Two & Three: Yuck!
Three: I'd rather starve!

One: I'm feeling a bit under the weather. You two go out without me.

Two: Without you! We can't have any fun if we're worrying about you all night.

One: No need to worry.

Three: You're telling us not to worry about you? What kind of cold, callous people do you think we are?

Two: Yeah, you've got some nerve thinking we could go out and have a good time when you're feeling under the weather.

One: It's really nothing. I'm just a little tired. No reason to spoil your evening on my account.

Two: It's nothing you say?

Three: Really nothing?

One: Well, nothing to worry about.

Two: So you've been making us worry for nothing?

Three: Do you think we appreciate having a hypochondriac ruin our evening?

One: Who's a hypochondriac? I just don't feel like going out.

Two: Oh, so you're not a hypochondriac. Then I guess you must be a liar!

Three: Telling tall tales to get out of going out with us!

One: You know, all of a sudden I'm starting to perk up a bit. Maybe I will go out after all.

Two: Yeah, well you can go out by yourself.

Three: Yeah. Count us out. You've already ruined our evening.

Two & Three: We're staying home!

One: Blue or green?

Two: What kind of question is that?

One: I'm trying to decide what color shirt to wear.

Two: Are blue and green the only choices.

One: I've limited myself to those choices. For today, at least.

Three: Is there a reason you're limiting yourself to blue or green? Why not red or orange?

One: That would be impossible. I don't own an orange shirt.

Two: Well, how about red or green?

Three: Actually, why even limit yourself to two? Why not red or green or blue?

One: You're making things more difficult for me.

Two: Why do you always avoid the difficult decisions?

One: Believe me, blue or green is difficult enough.

Two: Difficult? It's easy. Blue, of course.

Three: Green!

Two: Green? That's ridiculous!

Three: Look who's talking. Blue. Ha!

One: Let me know when you two have come to a consensus.

One: I'm at the end of my rope.

Three: What's the problem?

One: It's the bureaucracy.

Two: The bureaucracy can be a pain.

One: You're telling me!

Three: So what's the problem?

One: I told you, the bureaucracy.

Three: Yes, but what are you trying to do that the bureaucracy is preventing you from doing?

One: That's the problem! I can't even find out.

One: One, two, three, five, six, seven.

Two: You forgot four.

One: What makes you think I forgot four?

Two: Because you didn't say it.

One: Why should I say it?

Two: Because you were counting by ones and you left four out.

Three: Yes, I noticed that too, though I wasn't going to say anything.

One: Well, you're both making quite an assumption.

Two: It was a natural assumption.

Three: Yes, totally natural.

One: Natural perhaps, but wrong. I wasn't counting at all. I was merely vocalizing random numbers.

Two: Random! They hardly sounded random to me.

Three: Yes, they sounded quite deliberate and sequential. Except for the missing four, that is.

One: Well, the missing four is the key. It's proof that my numbers were random. Randomness sometimes masquerades as order, but there's always something, in this case the absence of the number four, that exposes it for the randomness it is.

Two: Wait a minute. You chose those numbers. You chose the sequence. You chose to leave out four. I'd hardly call that randomness.

One: What would you call it?

Two: Gee, I don't know.

Three: I know what I'd call it. I'd call it pulling a fast one.

One: All right, that's fine with me. As long as you don't call it counting.

One: I have a phantom pain where my leg used to be.

Two: What are you talking about?

Three: Yeah, what do you mean? You still have both of your legs.

One: Yes, but an hour ago my legs were elsewhere. They were in the other room.

Two: What are you talking about?

One: An hour ago I was in the other room, hence my legs were in the other room. And now I'm feeling a phantom pain in the other room. Where my left leg was.

Three: Wait a minute. You're feeling a phantom pain in another room?

One: Yes.

Two: I've never heard of anything like that before.

Three: Yeah, this is one for the medical journals.

Two: Should we call a neurologist?

One: No, that won't be necessary.

Three: Won't be necessary? How come?

One: I've got it all figured out.

Two: You do? So what's the answer?

One: I'm going back to the other room to reclaim my pain.

∾

One: I'm in a rut. My ruminations have become predictable. They're hardly worthy of the name "ruminations" any more.

Two: Sounds like you need a rumination makeover.

One: Precisely.

Three: Why don't you take a hiatus from rumination? It might do you good.

One: You're suggesting a rumination vacation?

Three: I was thinking of it as a moratorium.

One: So basically my choices are a rumination makeover or a rumination moratorium?

Two & Three: It appears so.

One: I'll have to meditate on those options at length. Thanks! You've solved my problem.

Two: Where do you see yourself in five years?
One: Here. Five years older.
Three: What are your qualifications?
One: Time and immobility.
Two & Three: You're hired!

One: The sun is going to burn out in five billion years and there's nothing we can do about it.

Two: But there are many things of much more immediate concern that we do have power over.

One: Yes, but ultimately the sun is going to burn out, so what's the point of doing anything?

Three: That's a silly, illogical, defeatist attitude. Anyway, where do you think you'll be in five billion years?

One: Me? I have no idea where I'll be from one minute to the next.

Three: So why are you worrying about the sun burning out?

One: Worrying? Who's worrying? I take things one day at a time!

Two: It sure sounded like you were worrying.

One: I was just making a statement of scientific fact. But I don't have time to talk about it any longer. I've got to get out of here, and pronto.

Two & Three: Oh? Where are you going?

One: Out to get a tan, while I still have a chance.

One: I have a craving for New England clam chowder.

Two: I have a craving for Manhattan clam chowder.

Three: That's funny, so do I.

One: Have you ever noticed that neither of you ever shares my cravings?

Two: What do you mean? We both crave clam chowder, don't we?

One: Sure. Manhattan. I crave New England.

Three: You're blowing this all out of proportion. Manhattan, New England, what's the difference?

One: Cream, for one thing. Tomatoes for another.

Three: Small details. You should focus on our areas of agreement.

One: What would those be?

Two & Three: Clams and potatoes!

One: Never a dull moment.

Two: Something happen?

One: Something's always happening, wouldn't you say?

Two: That's undeniable, but I meant did something in particular happen that caused you to say, "Never a dull moment"?

One: Nothing in particular. No.

Three: Then why did you say it?

One: Why did I say, "Never a dull moment"? Is that what you're asking?

Three: Yes. Why did you say, "Never a dull moment"?

One: I don't know, really. I suppose I was bored.

Two: Are we free?

Three: We're not enslaved, if that's what you're asking.

One: Really? Sometimes I feel as if we're enslaved by each other.

Three: Does that bother you?

One: Not especially. As long as we're all enslaving each other in a fair and equitable manner, it's no worse than being free.

One: I'd like to make a film.
Two: What about?
One: About the three of us.
Three: Yes, but what about the three of us?
One: A day in the life of the three of us.
Two: Oh, a documentary?
One: No, I'd like it to be fiction.
Three: A fictional story about the three of us?
One: Yes.
Two: So, who would play us?
One: We'd play each other.
Three: Why don't we just play ourselves?
One: Are you kidding? Who'd pay to see that?

Two: Where have you been?

Three: Yeah, we haven't seen you for weeks.

One: I was abducted by aliens.

Three: That's terrible. Did they hurt you?

One: No.

Two: So what happened?

One: Not much. We basically just sat around talking.

Three: So, what did they look like?

One: Actually, they looked like you two.

One: I'm having a senior moment.

Two: Are you that old?

One: Old enough.

Three: You're of a certain age, I'll grant you that.

Two: But senior?

One: Not me, necessarily, but some of my moments for sure.

Three: So you're saying your moments are senior, regardless of your own personal seniority?

One: Essentially. A moment is very brief, and the life of a moment progresses from infancy to seniority quicker than you can say Jack Robinson.

Two: "Quicker than you can say Jack Robinson." I haven't heard that in ages!

Three: Ditto.

One: Funny, I hadn't intended to say that. It makes me wonder whether we're all older than we realize.

One: I once had dreams. Aspirations.

Two: What happened to them?

One: I suffered disappointment after disappointment.

Three: That's a shame. But you should never give up on your dreams. You never know when things might turn around.

One: But I've forgotten all my dreams and aspirations. I wouldn't know what to hope for any more.

Two: So hope for something new.

Three: Yes, never give up hope. It doesn't matter what you hope for, as long as you hope.

One: Thanks. You've given me hope. I now have a new aspiration. Everything's going to be different from here on in.

Two: So, what are you hoping for?

One: Disappointment.

One: I'm considering suicide.

Two & Three: It can't be as bad as that!

One: No, I'm considering it in the abstract, in case things ever get really bad.

Two: Are they good now?

One: Not especially, come to think of it.

Three: Is there any reason to go on living?

One: None that I can think of, now that you ask.

Two: So then you're really considering suicide?

One: Not at all.

Three: But you said if things ever got really bad you'd consider suicide.

One: They're already really bad. They've been really bad for as long as I can remember. Awful, as a matter of fact. Couldn't get much worse.

Three: So you're considering suicide?

One: Only in the abstract.

Two & Three: That's a relief!

One: So, how are you two doing?

Two & Three: Couldn't be better!

One: Do you smell something?

Two: Oranges?

Three: Death?

One: No, not oranges or death. I can't put my finger on it. It's a familiar smell, but somehow elusive.

Two: No, that definitely doesn't sound like oranges. The smell of oranges would be familiar, but hardly elusive.

Three: The smell of death could be elusive, though. It really depends on what one means by the smell of death.

Two: True. Are we talking about putrefaction, or that raw meat kind of smell?

Three: Or maybe something more abstract. Not necessarily the smell of the dead, but the smell of death itself, death the concept.

Two: But what would that smell be?

Three: It would be hard to put one's finger on.

Two: Could it be the smell of absence?

Three: Perhaps, but what would that be, exactly? Certainly not the absence of smell.

Two: It might be more like the mental image of a smell.

Three: Perhaps, but I'm not sure you could really call it an image.

Two: I was using "image" metaphorically.

Three: I see.

One: Wait…I've got it! Toasting marshmallows!

Two & Three: Hey, you're right!

∾

One: The Zoroastrians have the right idea.

Two: What's that?

One: Don't bury the dead. Leave the corpse in a tower for the vultures to pick clean.

Three: What if the vultures don't come?

One: The vultures always come!

One: Another day.

Two: Pretty much the same as yesterday.

Three: Pretty much the same as every day.

One: Yet different in its way. Different as any day is from all others.

Two: A unique day.

Three: A day unlike any other.

One, Two & Three: Another day!

A Certain Clarence

I

Clarence decided to paint his room. It was a small room, and Clarence reasoned that he could create the illusion of more space if he were to paint his room the colors of outside. So he painted his ceiling blue like the sky, with a couple of white clouds for good measure. He painted his floor in patches of green and brown, like grass and earth. And his walls he painted no color at all.

II

Clarence was trying to find the right word, the mot juste, to complete the thought he was thinking. He tried all sorts of words, but none of them was any good. "Goose" didn't do the trick, nor did "walking" nor "handkerchief." For one thing, the word he needed was more along the lines of a concept. Like "freedom," but not quite. And not "envy" and not "cowardice" and not "time." Clarence went on like this for hours. He would consider a word, then discard it. "Ineptitude" wouldn't work, nor would "libertinism." "Heat," "justice," and "nothing-ness" were all out of the question. Thousands of words proved "inappropriate." But Clarence, never one to accept "defeat," continued his search. For days he auditioned words, giving up sleep, missing meals. And by the time he finally came upon the right word, which happened to be "infallibility," Clarence could no longer remember the rest of the thought he had been thinking.

III

Clarence had forgotten it was a leap year until almost the last minute. He woke up on February 28 and realized that it was not the last day of the month. This realization greatly disturbed Clarence. This year had an extra day and he had not accounted for it; he was not prepared. What would he do with it, this day he hadn't counted on? Clarence was so upset that he couldn't get out of bed. He was paralyzed. How could he have forgotten? Moron, he called himself. He wanted to punch himself. But he didn't. He just lay in bed all day, agonizing. And as midnight approached Clarence noticed that he had lost an entire day worrying about tomorrow. At which point he congratulated himself, smiled, and went to sleep.

IV

Clarence got a phone call. "Hello, is Clarence there?"

"Yes, this is Clarence," Clarence replied.

"Clarence Johnson?"

"No, I'm afraid you have the wrong number," Clarence replied and hung up.

Later that day, Clarence got another phone call. "Hello, is this Clarence?"

"Yes." Clarence replied.

"Clarence Fong?"

"No, I'm afraid not," Clarence replied and hung up.

The next day Clarence's phone rang. He picked it up on the third ring. "Clarence?"

"Yes."

"Clarence Moskowitz?"

"No," Clarence replied and hung up.

That week, Clarence got calls for Clarence Swenson, Clarence Masterson, Clarence Hume, Clarence Landesman, Clarence Washington, Clarence McPhee, and Clarence LeBoeuf.

Funny, Clarence thought, all these Clarences and none of them me.

V

His apartment was dark and gloomy, so Clarence bought a lamp and called it a window. He placed it at the far end of his room and, hearing an imaginary drumroll, he flipped the switch, but nothing happened—still dark. Frustrated but far from defeated, he went out again and bought a squeegee. He returned home and began to squeegee the lamp, with his eyes closed, and imagined as he squeegeed that the world outside was beginning to come through, slowly but surely, little by little. In his mind's eye he saw trees and houses and sky and even Mr. Aho from across the street, but when he opened his eyes—still dark. Depressed and despondent, he sat in his favorite and only chair and stared into space, a space he could hardly see. And then, two hours later, all of a sudden, the sun began to shine for the first time in months, through his windows, the other windows, that is, the windows that weren't lamps, the windows he had forgotten were there, and with this light came a revelation, for the light shone brightly upon his lamp and he could see now what he could not see before—that his lamp was without a bulb. This realization made Clarence laugh and cry simultaneously—he had bought a lamp without a bulb, silly Clarence, a windowless window he no longer needed, at least as long as present conditions prevailed.

VI

Clarence went to a sex shop and purchased an inflatable love doll. He brought the doll home and blew it up. He named it Eve and decided that his apartment was the Garden of Eden before the fall. After that Clarence couldn't remember why he had bought the doll.

A Certain Clarence

VII

Clarence was watching a war on the evening news when it began to escalate and spilled over into his living room. How inconvenient, Clarence thought, I was hoping for a quiet evening at home. Clarence tried to ignore the soldiers and go about his business. He ate a tuna sandwich and read forty-seven pages of Proust as the war raged on. The presence of so many strangers in his apartment made him uncomfortable, but he had no intention of being forced out of his own home. At 11:30 he changed into his pajamas. He tried to get into the bathroom, to brush his teeth, but a General slammed the door in his face. "It's occupied," the General said. So Clarence went to bed, teeth unbrushed, mad as hell. He tried to fall asleep, but the war was making too much noise — incessant gunfire, grenades exploding all over the apartment, soldiers shouting foul epithets at each other. Finally, Clarence gave up. There was no way he'd get a minute's sleep if he stayed at home, so he abandoned his apartment and booked himself into a nearby hotel. By morning the war had spread to other apartments, and by the end of the second day all the tenants in Clarence's building had been displaced by war.

VIII

Clarence would like to discover the answer to an age-old question, so he goes to a restaurant and orders two items: a roast chicken, and one egg, scrambled. The waiter, who is used to Clarence by now, does not balk at the order. Clarence, as always, awaits his lunch with nervous anticipation. He taps the table with his fingertips and looks at his watch numerous times. And then, after about fifteen minutes, his order arrives, the chicken and the egg, at the same time and on the same plate. Disappointed, he begins to eat. I don't know why I keep coming back, Clarence thinks. You never get any answers.

IX

Clarence bought a do-it-yourself kit, on sale. He didn't know what it was a kit for, as all the writing on the package was in a foreign language he didn't understand, but the price was right, so he bought it. When he returned home from the store, Clarence opened the package and, as he suspected, the instructions were in the same foreign language. But that wasn't all—other than the instruction sheet, there was nothing in the box. Clarence was annoyed, but he was also intrigued. Now, more than before, he had to know what the instructions said—he wasn't about to throw two dollars out the window. So he went to the library with the instruction sheet. He assumed the language was Asian, as the script itself was unfamiliar, so he went straight to the Asian languages section and started perusing the books on the shelves. Before long Clarence discovered that the language was Tamil. That was the easy part. The hard part was learning the language. Clarence spent many months teaching himself Tamil, and when he was confident he had mastered the rudiments of the language he once again looked at the instruction sheet. But the "instructions" gave no clue as to how to make anything. In fact, the sheet consisted of nothing more than several short passages, with such titles as "School Days," and "Loyalty," written in the simple style of a child's primer, followed by one word at the bottom of the sheet, the Tamil equivalent of "congratulations." Clarence finally understood what was going on when he looked again at the box that the instructions had come in and translated the big red letters, the name of the kit: "TEACH YOURSELF TAMIL."

X

Clarence was experiencing an emotion he couldn't place; an unfamiliar emotion. An emotion which, as far as he could remember, he had never previously experienced. It was an emotion unlike any he could give a name to. It was nothing like being in love, bore no relation to envy, and in no way approached the ballpark of sadness. An unknown emotion, an indescribable one. Yet this emotion, and its very inscrutability, was becoming the impetus for other emotions, utterly familiar ones, like frustration, confusion, and fear. In fact, these emotions became so intense that Clarence no longer even noticed the original emotion, the one that was the cause of these other ones, these run-of-the-mill emotions. Clarence was relieved. Never before had he so appreciated the emotions he knew.

XI

Clarence woke up in a cold sweat from his nightmare. In the nightmare, everybody who met Clarence called him by the wrong name. "I'm Clarence," he would insist, but they still called him by other names. Different names, all sorts of names. Strangers called him by the wrong name, but so did people he knew. His own mother called him General Grant, his father called him Mr. Tanaka, and his third grade teacher called him Mary Jane. Clarence was confused and alarmed, beside himself with angst. And then he woke up. Relieved to discover that it was all just a dream, Clarence took a few minutes to catch his breath and pull himself together. Then he picked up the phone and called information, to find out how he was listed.

XII

Clarence went to a photographer's studio. "I would like you to shoot some baby pictures for me," Clarence told the photographer.

"Very well," the photographer said, "where's the baby?"

"I would like some baby pictures of myself," Clarence replied. "I don't have any baby pictures of myself."

"I don't have time for pranks. I'm a very busy photographer," the photographer told Clarence.

"I'm serious," said Clarence. "I would like some baby pictures of myself, and I'm prepared to pay you anything you ask."

Hmmm, the photographer thought, this man is obviously crazy, but who am I to turn down a paying job? "Very well," the photographer said, "I'll do it."

The photographer had all the props. For the first picture, Clarence had to remove all his clothes. It was the bearskin rug shot, and for this one Clarence smiled a smile that was startling in its innocence.

The next shot involved a baby bonnet, and as even the largest one the photographer could muster up was painfully tight, Clarence cried a cry that was remarkably babylike.

The third shot presented a problem. This one required a sailor's uniform, but there was no way Clarence would fit into any of the baby-sized ones in the photographer's studio. So the photographer sent out to the Army-Navy store for a Clarence-sized uniform. As soon as it arrived, Clarence tried it on—a perfect fit. As he watched the birdie, Clarence showed an expression of truly infantile fascination.

The photographer developed the photos while Clarence waited.

"Here they are," the photographer said, as he handed the pictures to Clarence. Three photographs of the adult Clarence in babylike poses.

"These are no good," Clarence said, angrily. "These aren't baby pictures. I won't take them."

The photographer wanted to kill Clarence, but he had an idea. "I have an idea," the photographer told Clarence, "but we'll have to shoot the photos again. And it's going to be expensive."

"Anything," Clarence said. "If you can shoot real baby pictures of me, I'll pay anything."

So the photographer did the same three shots again, the bearskin, the bonnet, and the sailor.

But this time, instead of developing these, the photographer substituted three photos of a real baby in the same poses. He showed them to Clarence.

"Wonderful! Just wonderful," Clarence said, elated. "It's me as a baby! How much do I owe you?"

The photographer named an exorbitant price, which Clarence gladly paid. He left the studio an extremely happy man.

The photographer was very happy too. In addition to the large fee he extracted from Clarence, he sold the original photos of Clarence to a magazine that pays handsomely for such oddities.

XIII

Clarence bought a map of the world, and using this map as a guide, he tried to extrapolate a map of his room. He soon discovered that this task would not be as easy as he had first imagined. For the map he had purchased was a contemporary map, a map of the world as we know it today. This was all good and well, but Clarence knew that this was not the first map of the world. This map was the result of thousands of years of mapmaking and an ever-changing world. Clarence's map, on the other hand, would be the first of his room, without precedent. He could only map it as he saw it, as he knew it, but he knew that this would be seen as a crude representation by future generations. Of course, he would be hailed as a pioneer by some, but those who knew better would also find much to scoff at. Clarence decided he'd rather not have his faults so brazenly exposed, so he abandoned the project. However, now haunted by the knowledge that he was without a map of his room, he started bumping into things at every turn, until he was left with no choice but to move to another room and start afresh.

XIV

It was a wild idea, but Clarence decided to write a play, about himself, called "The Importance of Being Clarence." The play would have only one character, Clarence, but it wouldn't be a monologue—it would be a dialogue, between the fictional Clarence, the Clarence in the play and the other Clarence, the real Clarence, that is, the writer, the one who, hey, where did he go?

XV

Short on cash, Clarence realized he'd have to make a living, or at least get a job. He perused the want ads but didn't see anything suitable, so he figured he'd just have to pound the pavement. Clarence wasn't quite sure how pounding the pavement could lead to a job, but he had always heard that this is how it's done.

Clarence had no idea what one should use to pound the pavement, so he decided to try a judge's gavel. He got down on his hands and knees on one of the busiest streets of his city and began to pound the pavement with the gavel. A crowd gathered around him.

"What are you doing?" someone asked.

Perhaps it's not as evident as I had thought, Clarence thought. Not wanting to make a fool of himself by saying, "I'm pounding the pavement," Clarence replied, "It's the day of judgment, and I'm judging the city."

Some figured he was a religious fanatic, and they walked away. Some thought he was just a garden-variety nut case, and they walked away. The rest, however, assumed he was a performance artist, and they began to shower him with money.

Clarence was pleased. So, pounding the pavement really does pay off after all, he told himself.

XVI

Atop a table in Clarence's apartment was an object without a name. The object, whatever it was, could not be described, as all of its properties and qualities were utterly inexpressible in terms of any known language. Now you might think this would disturb Clarence, but nothing could be further from the truth. In fact, Clarence never knew the thing was there.

XVII

If you asked Clarence, on any particular day, "What was the first word that came into your mind this morning?" he would most likely tell you he didn't remember, unless, of course, that particular day happened to be last Tuesday. For last Tuesday was the day that Clarence awoke thinking, "Clarence." He had his own name on his mind, and it must have started while he was still asleep, because it was right there, firmly there, when he woke up. "Clarence"—it felt strange, to wake up with his own name. What was it doing there, he wondered, his own name, dominating his thoughts, like an uninvited guest? "Clarence"—Clarence couldn't get the word, the name, out of his mind. What's this all about, he wondered, disturbed, unsettled. And just what was this "Clarence" he was thinking? Was it he, Clarence himself, that he couldn't stop thinking about, or was it just his name, a sound, "Clarence?" The more he thought about it, the more unsettled he became, and as he kept repeating the name, the sound, the idea, "Clarence," he began to doubt his own identity. He could no longer reconcile his being with the sound of his own name. He began to doubt that Clarence was his name. How could he be Clarence? Clarence was just a nonsense word, signifying nothing, or, if not quite nothing, certainly not him. He began to imagine other uses for the word "Clarence." Clarence: A vessel for storing perishable foodstuffs. Clarence: A small flowering plant indigenous to the South Pacific. Clarence: Clarence: Clarence: And if he wasn't Clarence, then who was he? He went on like this for hours, tormenting himself, trying to make sense of the word "Clarence" and of himself. But finally, happily, thankfully, he was saved by another idea, a brainstorm. This word he had been thinking, this name, this "Clarence," did not necessarily apply to him in the first place. After all, there were plenty of other Clarences in this world. Perhaps the name with which he awoke, the word, was the name of another Clarence, another person. Another person's name. Another human being. And with this revelation, Clarence, by taking the word that had dominated his thoughts that morning, the name, and applying it to another human being, another entity, was at last able to get it off his mind and, by doing so, had begun to feel himself once again—Clarence.

XVIII

Clarence went to the doctor. He needed to get the requisite inoculations for his vacation, a trip to the dustball in the corner of his room. The doctor gave him a shot of house dust serum and prescribed some antihistamines. "Are you sure you want to make this trip?" the doctor asked. "It doesn't sound like much fun."

"It's more for education than relaxation," Clarence replied. "I'm curious."

It was a large dustball. Clarence had let it accumulate with a visit specifically in mind. He went to the dustball on Saturday morning, planning to spend the weekend. A dustball is the perfect place for a short excursion—there's not much to do in one, but it's worth a look, or so the guidebook had said.

For the trip Clarence wore a pair of jeans and an old sweatshirt. The guidebook, *Dustballs on Pennies a Day*, said, "No need to pack a jacket and tie. In a dustball, casual is the word."

The dustball was revolting, but it was cheap. As Clarence walked around he noticed hair, and crumbs and dirt of various kinds, a few dead cockroaches, and, of course, plenty of house dust. The antihistamines made him sleepy, so he lay down in the dust for a nap.

Clarence had a dream. It was an erotic dream, of the frustrating variety. In the dream, Botticelli's Venus arose from the dust. "You look familiar," Clarence said. "Aren't you Botticelli's

Venus?" But the woman didn't answer. Clarence was quite aroused, and he began to caress the nude apparition, planting kisses all over her face and breasts.

"Not here," she finally said. "Dirty!"

"But you came from the dust," Clarence said, imploringly.

"Dirty, dirty, dirty," she said, and crumbled to dust.

When Clarence woke up he didn't remember the dream. But he was seized with a fascination for house dust, and he once again began to wander. Dust everywhere. Venice has canals, Paris has bridges, and dustballs have dust. Clarence was intoxicated by the dust. Transfixed, he sat down and wondered, why does dust have this powerful effect on me? He began to thumb through the guidebook and came upon a section entitled "The Composition of House Dust." He read, "The greater portion of house dust is composed of particles of dead human skin." There was Clarence's answer: As he never had visitors to his apartment, this house dust was, for the most part, his own dead skin. He cut his trip short and left the dustball, for that was all he needed to know.

Outside the dustball but still in his room, Clarence coughed and thought, I have made the journey and I have found myself.

XIX

Clarence awoke one morning to discover that the floor of his bedroom had turned to mud. Bleary eyed, he stepped out of bed and experienced a startling sensation. Beneath his feet was not the dry, plush carpet that he expected, that he counted on. No, his bare feet had touched something wet, something wet and thick. Clarence looked down and saw that his entire floor was covered with mud—wall-to-wall mud, deep brown mud.

I must get to the bottom of this, Clarence thought. So he took off his pajamas, not wanting to stain them, and got down on his hands and knees. Naked in the mud, Clarence began to dig, using only his bare hands. There was something he had to find out, one important detail, one essential fact. So he dug furiously, heart racing, adrenaline pumping. He dug like a man possessed. He dug and dug until he was certain that it would be pointless to dig any further, until he had ascertained that there was no carpet beneath the mud, only soil and stone— terra firma. And then, suddenly calm, he got up, walked over to the window, opened the curtains, and gazed out at a familiar world he no longer recognized.

XX

Clarence decided he needed a hobby, so he took up topiary gardening. He proved to be a natural. Like an old pro, he cut the shrubs of his garden in the most amazing shapes. First there were the farm animals, then the gargoyles, then five American Presidents of the mid-nineteenth century—Polk, Taylor, Fillmore, Pierce and Buchanan. But soon there were more complex shapes, the shapes of pain, love, grief, hunger and happiness, to name just a few. Quite a garden, to say the least, but only a beginning, as far as Clarence was concerned. Clarence had one more shrub in mind, the shrub to end all shrubs, his life's work, the shrub he is cutting right now, the shrub he keeps cutting, keeps shaping, cutting and shaping, shaping and cutting—the shrub in the shape of death.

XXI

One day, Clarence was browsing through a bookstore at a mall when he was startled to discover a book, a big fat book, in which he was the main character. He stood there, in the store, for hours, reading this book. It was amazing—the writer had captured his entire life, down to the most minute detail. It even seemed as though the writing itself, the style and texture of the prose, brilliantly captured the flavor of what it was like to be Clarence. Clarence was enthralled. Finally, just as he was getting to the part about today, the proprietor approached him and said, angrily, "What do you think this is—a library?"

"No sir," Clarence replied.

"In that case," the proprietor said, "buy it or put it back."

Of course he couldn't put it back—he wanted to read about today, and especially tomorrow. So he bought it. It cost him an arm and a leg, but he bought it.

Clarence returned home and resumed where he had left off. When he had finished the part about today, he was all ready to read about tomorrow and, it seemed, a multitude of tomorrows, for there must have been thousands of pages left—the author had obviously been paid by the word. But when Clarence turned the page something odd happened—he was now at the back cover of the book. Yet the book was just as thick as before. Something must have gone wrong, he figured, so he tried again. He went back to the page about today and turned the page, carefully, but once again he reached the back cover. He tried this several more times, all to the same end. This book is defective, he thought, and he decided to return it. So he left his apartment and ran, with the big book under his arm, back to the bookstore, but when he got there the bookstore was gone. Well, Clarence thought, I guess there are some things you just can't return.